TIME HOP SWEETS SHOP
Cookies with Clara Barton

By Kyla Steinkraus

Illustrated by Sally Garland

Rourke
Educational Media
rourkeeducationalmedia.com

www.rourkeeducationalmedia.com

Edited by: Keli Sipperley
Cover and Interior layout by: Tara Raymo
Cover and Interior Illustrations by: Sally Garland

Library of Congress PCN Data

Cookies with Clara Barton / Kyla Steinkraus
(Time Hop Sweets Shop)
ISBN (hard cover)(alk. paper) 978-1-68191-370-4
ISBN (soft cover) 978-1-68191-412-1
ISBN (e-Book) 978-1-68191-453-4
Library of Congress Control Number: 2015951482

Printed in the United States of America,
North Mankato, Minnesota

Dear Parents and Teachers,

Fiona and Finley are just like any modern-day kids. They help out with the family business, face struggles and triumphs at school, travel through time with important historical figures ...

Well, maybe that part's not so ordinary. At the Time Hop Sweets Shop, anything can happen, at any point in time. The family bakery draws customers from all over the map–and all over the history books. And when Tick Tock the parrot squawks, Fiona and Finley know an adventure is about to begin!

These beginner chapter books are designed to introduce students to important people in U.S. history, turning their accomplishments into adventures that Fiona, Finley, and young readers get to experience right along with them.

Perfect as read-alouds, read-alongs, or independent readers, books in the Time Hop Sweets Shop series were written to delight, inform, and engage your child or students by making each historical figure memorable and relatable. Each book includes a biography, comprehension questions, websites for further reading, and more.

We look forward to our time travels together!

Happy Reading,
Rourke Educational Media

Table of Contents

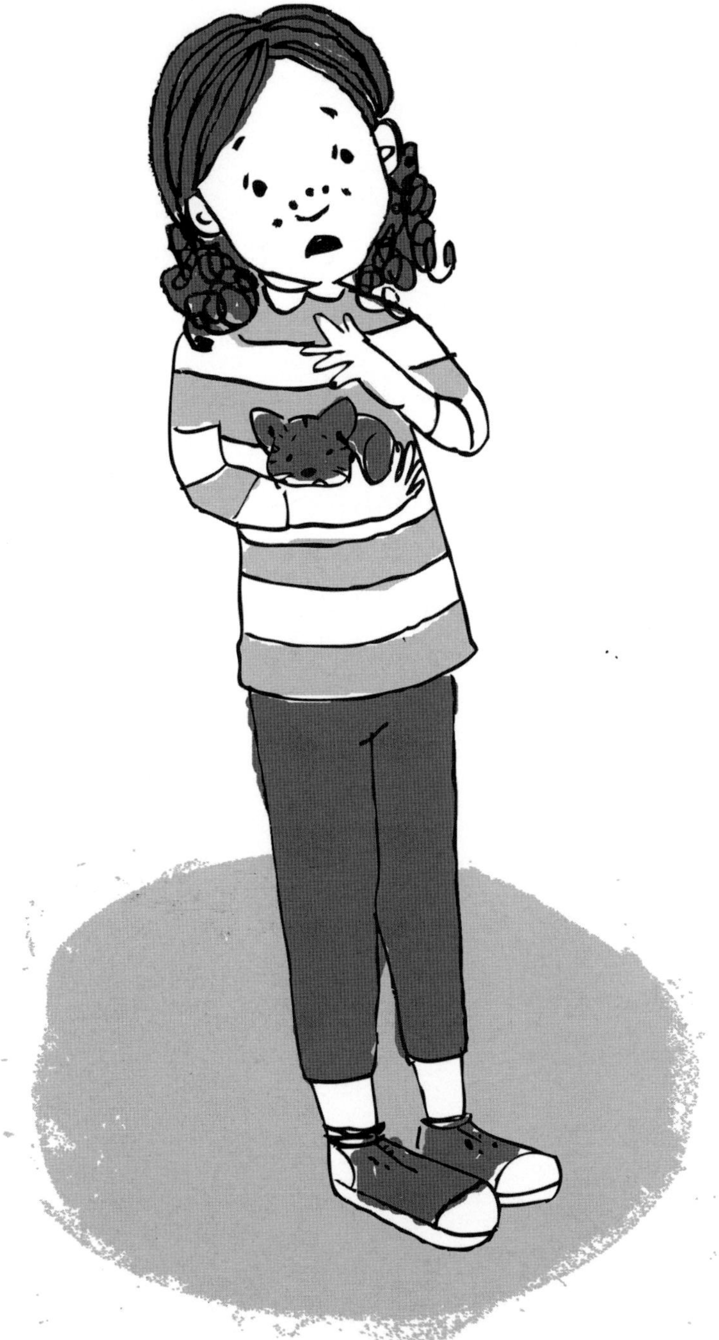

Chapter 1
Fiona to the Rescue

Fiona dashed into the Sweets Shop cradling something in her hands.

"What's that?" Finley asked. He was working behind the counter, making his favorite chunky chocolate chip cookies.

Finley and Fiona loved helping Mom and Dad after school. The Sweets Shop was special because it had desserts from different time periods, like cider cake, lemon gingerbread, and rhubarb tarts.

"Help me!" Fiona said. She was a whole year younger than Finley, but she was just as tall. She sometimes thought this made her the boss. Finley didn't agree.

Finley crossed his arms. "Why should I?"

She opened up her fingers. She was holding a tiny kitten! It meowed sadly.

"There's blood on its fur!" Finley said.

"It's a boy," Fiona said. "I already named him Twinkle Toes. Quick, get a damp washcloth. And get Dad!"

Usually Finley pretended his hearing aids were turned down when his sister told him what to do. This time he listened.

Finley brought the washcloth. Dad brought in some special medicine to put on the kitten's scratched leg. "The cut isn't too bad," Dad said, petting Twinkle Toes' head.

"He needs water," Fiona said. Finley couldn't find a bowl, so he filled a measuring cup with water. The tiny kitten lapped it up.

"I'll call Mom," Dad said. "She can pick up some milk from the store."

"Can we keep him? Pretty please?" Fiona and Finley asked together.

Dad laughed, holding up his hands. "I'm not making any promises!"

Just then Tick Tock, their parrot, flapped his wings. "Look at the time! Look at the time!" He squawked from his perch by the side door.

Fiona and Finley looked up, excited. A special visitor was coming!

The bell over the side door jingled as a woman walked in. She was a tiny lady, with a long dark skirt and dark hair pulled back into a bun. She smiled. "Hello! I heard this place makes the best cookies around."

"Oh, yes!" Fiona said, jumping up from her stool. "We're making some right now. Only my batch got burned because I was busy rescuing this baby kitten."

"Oh, my goodness!" the woman said. "May I see?"

Fiona showed the woman the fuzzy kitten. She explained how they had taken care of Twinkle Toes.

"Excellent work," the woman said. "That's exactly what I would have done."

"Are you a veterinarian?" Fiona asked.

"No," she said. "Although when I was young, my neighbors would bring their sick pets to me to take care of. I mostly take care of people."

"Are you a nurse, then?" Fiona asked.

"People call me a nurse. There weren't any trained nurses in my day."

Finley scrunched up his face. She did look very familiar. "Are you Clara Barton?"

"Yes, I am!" Clara Barton smiled.

Finley handed her a plate with two cookies and a glass of milk. "You lived during the Civil War! You cared for soldiers who were wounded in the fighting."

"Did you work in a hospital?" Fiona asked.

Clara shook her head. "No. I started out volunteering in the hospital in Washington, D.C., just as the war started. But it took days for the wounded soldiers to be carried in wagons from the battlefield to a hospital. There were not enough doctors to care for them or even to give them food and water.

That's when I knew. It was up to me to go to the battlefield myself to help them."

Finley gulped. "You weren't scared?"

Clara laughed and took a big bite of cookie. "I was terrified! I was scared of so many things. I was shy. But whenever anyone needed my help, my fear disappeared. I wanted to do good, to help others in any way I could."

"I want to help people, too!" Fiona said.

"Me too!" Finley said, but his stomach did an uneasy flip flop. He wanted to be helpful, but he didn't like to be scared.

Clara set down her plate. "I can always use more helpers. I stopped by for a quick bite to eat, but there is so much more work to do. Would you like to come with me to Fairfax, Virginia? The date is September 1, 1862. This battle will one day be known as the second Battle of Bull Run. Many good men have been killed. Many more are wounded."

Mom came in the front door of the Sweets Shop with a bag full of groceries.

"Can we go help, Mom? Pretty please?" Fiona asked.

Mom put down the groceries and shook Clara Barton's hand. "Of course. Just stick together, and stay out of danger."

Finley and Fiona looked at each other. They'd gotten in a few dangerous time hopping situations before, but they kept those stories to themselves. Usually they didn't know they were heading into trouble.

Finley followed Clara and Fiona to the side door. He felt nervous and scared. Could he be brave like Clara Barton?

Chapter 2
Angel of the Battlefield

"No time to waste!" Tick Tock cawed. The room began to spin and whirl. It felt like doing lots of cartwheels.

That was the worst part of time hopping for Finley. It was the best part for Fiona. They landed hard on their bottoms in the dirt.

Finley's shorts and T-shirt had changed into a white shirt tucked into suspenders and uncomfortable, old fashioned shoes. Fiona wore a long dark dress like Clara's.

Fiona and Finley blinked in the bright sunlight and looked around.

They were in a field surrounded by trees on a hillside. Everywhere they looked, men lay on the hay-covered ground. They wore old fashioned blue uniforms. They were all wounded or sick.

There were sounds like big and small explosions all around them.

"What's that noise?" Finley asked, his heart thumping in his chest.

"That is cannon and musket fire," Clara said. "Muskets are old fashioned guns."

Fiona covered her face with her hands. "This is terrible!"

"War is terrible," Clara said. "These men are fighting for their country, the United States of America. These are Union soldiers. The southern soldiers are called Confederates. Before the Civil War, many people in the South had slaves, people who were forced to work all the time without pay or freedom. The North is fighting to free the slaves and keep the United States together."

At the edge of the field, soldiers in wagons brought more and more wounded men.

"There must be thousands!" Finley said.

"Yes," Clara said. "Three thousand wounded men. And eight thousand dead. While our soldiers can stand and fight, then we can stand and feed and nurse them, don't you think?"

"Yes!" Fiona cried. "Tell us what to do."

Clara led them to a spot with a small fire and two black kettles. "We must get the soldiers food and water. There isn't much, but even a little will keep them alive. Then we wash their wounds and give them fresh bandages."

She handed Fiona a bucket full of water and a small tin cup. "Can you give our guests a bit to drink?"

Then she showed Finley how to make soup to feed the soldiers. "Crush up the army biscuits. Then add some wine, water, and brown sugar," she said. "We only have four plates and five cups, can you believe it? Every time we use up a jar of preserves or container of food, we will save it and use it as a dish."

Finley looked at all the hurt soldiers who needed his help. He decided that if Clara wasn't scared, then he wouldn't be either. He had an important job to do.

Fiona and Finley walked among the rows and rows of soldiers. Fiona knelt down and gave each soldier water to drink. Some were so sick that Fiona had to hold the cup for them. When the bucket was empty, Fiona went back for more water.

One young soldier had his arm in a sling that Clara made for him. Finley served him some soup. "I haven't eaten for three days," the soldier said. "Thank you."

"What is your name?" Finley asked.

The yellow-haired soldier smiled. "Charley Hamilton. I know Miss Barton. She used to be my teacher."

"Clara Barton was a teacher?"

"Oh, yes." The soldier winced in pain. Finley gave him more soup to eat. "She was the best teacher I ever had. Now she is the best nurse I ever had. They call her the Angel of the Battlefield."

Finley watched Clara as she hurried among the men. She smiled at them. She held their hands. She talked to them as she bandaged up their wounds. "You must not give up," she said over and over.

She really did look just like an angel.

Chapter 3
So Much to be Done!

By the time Fiona and Finley had given away all of their food and water, it was nearly dark. Their legs were sore and their arms were tired. Their heads ached, but Finley and Fiona did not want to rest. There was so much more to be done! They asked Clara what else they could do.

She was writing a list of the soldier's names. She paused, wiping her face with the back of her sleeve.

"Miss Barton, what is that hole in your sleeve?" Fiona asked.

"Oh, that. I was leaning over to help a wounded soldier, and a bullet went right through my dress!"

Finley's face went white. He thought he might faint right there in the dirt.

"Don't worry, my boy." Clara patted Finley's arm. "I am still in one piece! I have too much to do to waste time getting shot."

"Did you ever get hurt?" Fiona asked.

"I had many close calls, but I was never hurt. Although, I did get sick several times because I couldn't take time to rest. I was at nearly every major battle during the Civil War."

Fiona picked up a lantern and held it up in the dark. "What will you do when the war ends?"

"I will create an organization to help families find out what happened to their missing soldiers. Over a four-year period, I will help find out what happened to more than twenty-two thousand missing men."

"Wowza," Fiona whispered.

"And then, when I am sixty years old, I

will start the American Red Cross," Clara said. "The Red Cross helps soldiers during wars. It also helps people during natural disasters, like floods and hurricanes."

"I know about the Red Cross," Finley said. "They still help people!"

"I know," Clara said proudly. "Thank you so much for your help. I think it's time for you two to go home now."

"But there's so much more to do!" Fiona cried.

"I know. I have pledged all that I have to the cause of justice and mercy. You can do the same thing, at home in your time. Take care of that kitten for me. Goodbye!" Clara Barton hugged Fiona and Finley, then the world began to swirl and spin.

A few seconds later, Fiona and Finley stumbled through the side door of the Sweets Shop.

"In the nick of time!" Tick Tock squawked.

Fiona and Finley looked at each other. "We have our freedom because of those brave soldiers," Finley said quietly.

"How can we be more like Clara Barton?" Fiona asked. She carefully picked up the kitten. Twinkle Toes purred happily. He would be okay!

"Who's hungry?" Dad asked, patting his apron.

"I have an idea," Finley said. "Dad, can we volunteer for the Red Cross?"

Dad smiled. "Of course you can. You can visit a veteran's hospital or help raise funds for disaster relief. Or you can write letters to soldiers stationed overseas."

Finley grinned at Fiona. "Yes to all of those! I think Clara Barton would be proud!"

Fiona nestled Twinkle Toes against her cheek. "Yes, I think she would be!"

About Clara Barton

Clara Barton was born on December 25, 1821, in North Oxford, Massachusetts. She had four much older brothers and sisters. They taught her to read and write when she was only four years old. As a girl, she was very shy. She was afraid of snakes and  thunderstorms. She hid when something was bothering her. Still, she grew up riding horses, reading, learning geography, and writing letters.

When she was eleven, her brother became ill after a fall. Clara nursed him day and night for two years. She enjoyed being useful and helping. At age seventeen, she became a teacher and taught in many schools. She established a free school for poor children. After ten years, she became the first female clerk in the U.S. Patent office.

When the Civil War began in 1861, Clara wanted to help. Women were not allowed to be soldiers. "If I can't be a soldier, I'll help soldiers," she said. She brought wagons filled with food, bandages, medicine, soap, and clothing to the battlefield. She bathed, fed, and bandaged the wounded soldiers.

After the war, she helped trace more than twenty thousand missing soldiers for their families. She gave lectures, telling stories of her experiences on the battlefield. While traveling in Europe, she learned about the International Red Cross, a group of volunteers who would nurse sick soldiers during wartime. In 1881, Clara founded the American Red Cross Society. She wanted to help soldiers and victims of national disasters. The Red Cross now has more than a half-million volunteers. Clara Barton died at the age of ninety on April 13, 1912.

Comprehension Questions

1. Why was Finley afraid to visit the Civil War?

2. Why did Clara Barton become a nurse?

3. How did Finley and Fiona help care for the soldiers?

Websites to Visit

www.clarabartonbirthplace.org

www.gardenofpraise.com/ibdbarto.htm

www.civilwar.org/education/history/
biographies/clara-barton.html

Q & A with Kyla Steinkraus

What most impressed you about Clara Barton?

She was extremely shy and fearful. But when she was helping someone else, she became fearless. She was brave and selfless in everything that she did.

Did you learn anything new in your research?

I learned so many things! I learned that Clara was a teacher for over ten years. I also learned that during Clara Barton's time, there were no trained nurses. She learned on the job.

What is your favorite part of Clara Barton's story?

When Clara first started teaching at the age of seventeen, several of her male students were not only her age, they were taller than she was, too. She quickly won their respect, however, when she could play ball better than they could!

About the Author

Kyla Steinkraus lives with her husband, two kids, and two spoiled cats in Atlanta, Georgia. She loves to create stories and characters. She also enjoys hiking, playing games, reading, and drawing. If she owned a Sweets Shop, she would only sell (and eat) chocolate!

About the Illustrator

Sally Anne Garland was born in Hereford England and moved to the Highlands of Scotland at the age of three. She studied Illustration at Edinburgh College of Art before moving to Glasgow where she now lives with her partner and young son.